The Adventures of Everyday Geniuses

Stacey Coolidge's FANCY-SMANCY Cursive Handwriting

Written by
Barbara Esham

Illustrated by
Mike & Carl Gordon

Published by Mainstream Connections, Perry Hall, MD

ISBN 9

© 2008,

Second grade started out so great.
I liked my teacher, Mrs. Thompson.
I liked my classroom.
And I especially liked Frederick, the class guinea pig.
I'd been waiting since first grade to be a big kid
and have the chance to play with him.

But my feelings changed during the third week of school —
the day we found the red folders. They were filled with
lined paper, and each of us was given a brand new pencil.
That was the day the word CURSIVE was mentioned.

"Class, today we will begin cursive handwriting exercises," Mrs. Thompson announced.

"Each day there will be three sentences that you must copy from the chalkboard. If you complete your handwriting early, you can read or work on the computer or play with Frederick."

That sounded good to me.
I would finally get a chance to play with Frederick.
He loved to be held, and he especially loved carrots for a treat.

I was still thinking about Frederick when Mrs. Thompson
said, "Everyone open your red folders and take
out one sheet of paper. We are going to start our handwriting
by practicing slants and curves.
We will then begin the letters of the alphabet."

I noticed each of my classmates was looking at their pencil
as if it was something new and mysterious
with special powers —
like a wizard's wand.

Even Frederick
looked nervous.

Then I heard Stacey Coolidge ask, "If we finish extra, extra early, can we play with Frederick AND work on the computer?"

"I don't think you need to worry about that right now, Stacey," Mrs. Thompson answered. "Each student will need plenty of time to practice cursive writing. If you should finish early, you can play with Frederick and work on the computer."

Stacey was the best at handwriting. She hardly ever used her eraser. I hoped Stacey wouldn't get to Frederick before I did...

I started by practicing my curves and slants, but I wasn't having much luck. I can color inside the lines of a picture and almost print my name inside the lines on notebook paper after a few tries. I can shoot a basket from where my big brother stands, and I can weave around cones with my skateboard without knocking a single one over.

How could writing a simple curve be so difficult? Writing sentences will probably be much easier.

It took us a while to learn all of our letters.
By then I realized that writing sentences wouldn't be
one bit easier than writing slants and curves.

One morning I asked my mom to take me to school early.
I wanted to get a head start so I could get a chance
to play with Frederick.

I was the first one to arrive.
Frederick was still
sleeping.

I pulled a fresh piece of paper from my red folder and started writing the first sentence from the board. I guess I was holding my pencil too tight, or maybe I was pressing too hard. For whatever reason, my first sentence didn't turn out too well.

Some of the words were too close together. I started to erase, but that made the worst smudge — like a storm cloud filling the sky.

When I tried to erase the gray storm cloud, I tore a hole in the paper.

9

One by one my classmates arrived. Everyone started working on the handwriting exercise. I was sure I would be the first one finished since I started before everyone else. Instead, I had a hole, some smudges, and a few worn spots on my paper, but I knew Mrs. Thompson would understand.

Some of the other kids were having a tough time too. Ben was almost finished when he realized that he was writing on the wrong lines. Mrs. Thompson asked him to start over with a fresh piece of paper.

That's when I saw Stacey Coolidge get up to turn in her paper.

She was finished!
How did she do it?

Then Mrs. Thomspson said, "Class, Stacey has finished her handwriting and I would like to share her work with the class.

Do you see how the curves of the **b** and **l** are perfectly slanted?

Notice how the **a** and **e** are just touching the center line?" Mrs. Thompson asked.

"Perfect, perfect, PERFECT!

Stacey Coolidge and her fancy smancy cursive handwriting," I said to myself quietly.

Why is everything so easy for Stacey?

It just doesn't seem fair.

And then Stacey did the unthinkable!

She walked right over to Frederick's cage and fed him a carrot. Then she had the nerve to put him in her lap! That's why I got here early! So I could feed Frederick a carrot and hold him in MY lap.

I could feel tears filling my eyes, but I held them back.

I still had to finish my cursive handwriting.

I was just finishing the last word when
Mrs. Thompson announced, "Time is up.
You can finish your work during recess if you like."

My paper looked like it was hundreds of years old – like one of
those important documents on display in the history museum.
I was embarrassed to hand it to Mrs. Thompson.

"Good try, Carolyn. I am sure cursive handwriting
will get easier for you. Maybe you can spend some more time
practicing at home."

I did practice at home, but it didn't seem to help. I just couldn't get my hand to cooperate with my brain. I knew what my handwriting was supposed to look like. I could see it in my mind, but my paper never looked that way when I was done.

How could cursive be so difficult?

After a few weeks of practicing, my cursive handwriting did get better — but not as good as everyone else's.

Mrs. Thompson made a bulletin board for all of her "Handwriting Stars." Everyone's paper was tacked to the bulletin board, but not everyone seemed like a star — at least not a star like Stacey Coolidge.

My handwriting was the **worst in the class,** on display for everyone to see.

17

Does Mrs. Thompson see how hard I'm working?

Does she see how many
erasers I've worn out?

Does she see the big bump
on the finger next to my thumb?

Will I ever be able to write
in cursive?

Will I get to go to the third grade?

Will I ever get to play with Frederick?

One day, Mrs. Thompson asked if she could speak to me after school. I was sure that she wanted to talk to me about my handwriting. I just knew it.

"Carolyn, you seem to be a bit sad lately. Is there something that you would like to talk about?" Mrs. Thompson asked.

"No Mrs. Thompson, I just don't know what to do about my handwriting. It's the worst in the class. I look at Stacey Coolidge's cursive handwriting, then I look at mine. Mine is terrible," I said with my shaky, "about to cry" voice.

"Carolyn, you are quite a smart little girl. I can see how hard you have been trying and I am so proud of you.

Cursive handwriting is something we need to practice. It is just a tool for our learning toolbox. If we have difficulty with one of our learning tools, we just find a different tool to work with," she said with one of her "serious" smiles.

"Some of the most talented poets and writers would have never had a chance if the most important part of their work was their cursive handwriting.

Ideas, thoughts, and feelings are the most important parts of what we write. Without the important parts, we just have a bunch of slants and curves."

21

"I have lots of ideas! And feelings! My dad always tells me that I have a great imagination!" I said, feeling much better.

"Promise me that you will let your wonderful imagination find a way into your writing," Mrs. Thompson said with her most serious look.

22 "Oh I promise, Mrs. Thompson!"

"Speaking of ideas – I think I have one of my own..."
said Mrs. Thompson.
"Let's celebrate Creative Writing in all its forms!"

"Now, there's another reason that I wanted to speak with you..."
said Mrs. Thompson, "I was wondering if you would consider
taking Frederick home with you for the weekend.
School will be closed on Monday
and I wouldn't want to
leave Frederick
alone for
that long."

"Really? For real?

I can take Frederick home with me for the whole weekend and Monday too?"

I couldn't believe it!

I'm really glad that Mrs. Thompson and I had a talk about cursive handwriting. I will always try my best, but I'm not going to feel bad about what my handwriting looks like. My ideas and imagination are the important things that will make my writing great. Who knows, maybe I'll even be a writer one day. Of course, I'll need to write in my spare time because I'll be very busy taking care of my very own...

...Guinea Pig Farm!

From Dr. Edward Hallowell,

New York Times national best seller, former Harvard Medical School instructor, and current director of the Hallowell Center for Cognitive and Emotional Health...

Fear is the great disabler. Fear is what keeps children from realizing their potential. It needs to be replaced with a feeling of I-know-I-can-make-progress-if-I-keep-trying-and-boy-do-I-ever-want-to-do-that!

One of the great goals of parents, teachers, and coaches should be to find areas in which a child might experience mastery, then make it possible for the child to feel this potent sensation.

The feeling of mastery transforms a child from a reluctant, fearful learner into a self-motivated player.

The mistake that parents, teachers, and coaches often make is that they demand mastery rather than lead children to it by helping them overcome the fear of failure.

The best parents are great teachers. My definition of a great teacher is a person who can lead another person to mastery.

~Dr. Hallowell

To read Dr. Hallowell's full letter, go to our website! Check out what ALL THE OTHER EXPERTS are saying about The Adventures of Everyday Geniuses book series. www.MainstreamConnections.org

A Note to Parents & Teachers

● ● ● ● ● ● ● ● ● ● ● ●

Mainstream Connections would like to help you help your kids become **Everyday Geniuses!**

These fun stories are an easy way to discuss learning styles and obstacles that can impede a child's potential.

The science of learning is making its way into the classroom! Everyday Geniuses are making their debut!

Call, email, or visit the website to learn how YOU can make a difference.

28   All books are available in bulk at discount for qualifying schools and professional organizations. Contact us!

The Adventures of Everyday Geniuses

RESOURCES for PARENTS and TEACHERS

The BIG LIST of resources can be found on our website. The big list is for parents and teachers, you know, just to give them the latest information on how our brains really learn, and what being smart is all about.

The topic of this book – Handwriting – is a learning obstacle for many Everyday Geniuses. Handwriting should never interfere with a child's intellectual or academic success. Alternate ways of expression and communication should always be explored.

Mainstream Connections provides you respected resources to help you create a happy, healthy learning environment for every child.

DOWNLOAD your complimentary Resource List today!

WEBSITES
Links to great sites to learn more about learning styles.

BOOK LISTS
Learn what the experts say about learning styles and obtacles.

CONNECT
News, info & support!

www.MainstreamConnections.org

The Mainstream Connections mission is to expose the broader definitions of learning, creativity, and intelligence. A substantial portion of all profits is held to fund and support the development of programs and services to give all children the tools needed for success.

Are you an EVERYDAY GENIUS TOO?

Get online with your favorite characters from

The Adventures of Everyday Geniuses

There is SO MUCH to do online!

- Meet the Gang and see what they are up to: ideas, inventions and algorithms, poems and other literary works, sEduardo's latest recipe, and get a list of great minds from the past and present!
- Download pages for coloring!
- Hats, Shirts, Classroom Stuff!

www.MainstreamConnections.org

Visit our website to learn more! Adults should always supervise children's web activity.

BOOK INFORMATION

Stacey Coolidge's Fancy-Smancy Cursive Handwriting
written by Barbara Esham illustrated by Mike & Carl Gordon

Published by Mainstream Connections Publishing
P.O. Box 398, Perry Hall Maryland 21128

Copyright © 2008, Barbara Esham. All rights reserved.

No part of this publication may be reproduced in whole or in part, in any form without permission from the publisher. *The Adventures of Everyday Geniuses* is a registered trademark.

Book design by Pneuma Books, LLC. www.pneumabooks.com

Printed in China ∞ Library Binding

FIRST EDITION

15 14 13 12 11 10 09 08   01 02 03 04 05 06 07 08

CATALOGING-IN-PUBLICATION DATA

Esham, Barbara.

Stacey Coolidge's fancy-smancy cursive handwriting / written by Barbara Esham ; illustrated by Mike & Carl Gordon. -- 1st ed. -- Ocean City, MD : Mainstream Connections, 2008.

p. ; cm.

(Adventures of everyday geniuses)

ISBN: 978-1-60336-462-1

Audience: Ages 5-10.

Summary: Carolyn has been practicing cursive handwriting, but is frustrated by her lack of success. Her classmate, Stacey Coolidge, has no problems with it, creating more self doubt for Carolyn. Carolyn's teacher finds a way to convince her that creative writing and cursive handwriting are two unrelated skills.

1. Penmanship--Juvenile fiction. 2. Creative ability in children--Juvenile fiction. 3. Anxiety--Juvenile fiction. 4. Self -esteem--Juvenile fiction. 5. Learning disabled children--Juvenile fiction. 6. Cognitive styles in children. 7. [Penmanship--Fiction. 8. Anxiety--Fiction. 9. Learning disabilities--Fiction.] I. Gordon, Mike. II. Gordon, Carl. III. Title. IV. Series.

PZ7.E74583 S73 2008   2007908046

[Fic]--dc22   0804